# SEEK TO TOUCH

*Seeking in Romance Book 2*

## KEKE RENÉE

304 Publishing Company

By Keke Renée:
Wet Heat
His Peace, Her Pleasure
Baby, It's Cold Outside
Love Don't Live Here Anymore, Book 1, 2
Every Time We Touch (A Wet Heat Novelette)
One Night Only-A Novelette - Love by Design Book 1
Cassian and Savannah - Love by Design Book 2
Deidra's Love - Love by Design Book 3
Protecting Bria (Special Forces Operation Alpha)
Haven
Taste
Sensual
Upcoming 2021
Seek To Please
Seek To Bare
Seek Touch
Seek To Bare

# INTRODUCTION

Are you signed up for my newsletter?

Join today and find out all the latest in new releases, contests, giveaways, sneak peeks and more.

https://landing.mailerlite.com/webforms/landing/r7j2s6

# DISCLAIMER

THIS WORK OF FICTION contains strong language and explicit sexual content and is only intended for mature readers. This story may contain unconventional situations, language, and sexual encounters that may offend some readers. I would recommend selecting another book. This book is for mature readers (18+).

SYNOPSIS

Lisa, a TV news anchor, is used to pressure at the job, but when she learns that someone is about to leak a video of her at a sex club, the pressure could make her life implode. If she doesn't do something to stop it, she'll lose her job, her family will disown her, and that's only the beginning.

Enlisting the help of her best friend's husband's business partner and security agent may be her only hope. If they can find out who is behind the scheme, her worries are over... she hopes.

Can they figure out who is out to ruin her before it's too late?

# LISA

It was ten at night, and a cool breeze flowed in Tennessee as my heels hit the gravel of the sidewalk in my new Stuart Weitzman custom shoes. I ordered them a week ago specifically for tonight. The black Andria strap heel paired perfectly with my off-the-shoulder short dress and side split. I had my hair pulled back in a bun with minimum makeup at his request. It wasn't like this was my first time; watching as Tony turned the lights off in the car parked down the street from my destination gave me comfort. He was Maya's security and driver, but she'd ask him if he'd accompany me whenever I made a trip over here. Looking from right to left, I raised my hand and knocked on the door, waiting to be let in like any other time. The place was mysterious, forbidden, and exotic to a regular person, but to me, it brought out a feeling of belonging. When Maya introduced this world, I hadn't looked back since. Once the door opened, I smiled to see my favorite bodyguard on duty tonight.

"Stephen."

"He's been waiting for you." Stephen helped to pull off my coat, and he whistled.

"Behave." I shook my index finger in front of his face.

"Never." He chuckled, and I giggled, shaking my head as I walked off down the long hallway of the entrance. I was grateful Maya had introduced me to Mason and allowed my entry into Club Seek. I was going on the fourth visit. I hadn't planned to stay too long since I needed to work early in the morning. As a reporter, our schedules changed if a breaking story popped up. As the head anchor, I had a duty to be ready and willing to get the correct information to the audience. Moving through the crowds, I took note of the new paintings Mason had hanging on the walls. The place still had the same old feel of a nightclub but an upscale adult lounge. Approaching the bar, I smiled at Sharon, who already had my drink ready for me before I even ordered. I was becoming a regular by now, or it probably had something to do with the person I was here to see.

"One apple martini." Sharon placed a fresh napkin next to the glass.

"How did you know this was the drink for the night?"

She winked, pointing over my shoulder.

"He wanted to make sure you were comfortable."

I lifted the glass and scanned the room when I noticed him standing near the crowd of couples huddled together in the corner. His watching me as I stared back gave me chills about what my night would entail.

"Don't keep him waiting too long."

Taking a sip turned into me gulping the entire martini down in one take. I nodded in response and placed it back on the counter.

"Thanks, Sharon."

Strolling through the crowd, a guy bumped into me, spilling a little of his drink on my dress.

"Shit, sorry about that." He tried to wipe the stain off.

"It's okay."

"No, let me buy you a new drink."

I felt a touch on my lower back, glanced behind me, and knew things would only get worse.

"The lady doesn't need you to buy her anything."

"My bad, Morris," the guy muttered, stepping back.

"She's with me."

I rolled my eyes; he always needed to be in control.

"It was an accident."

"Sorry again."

"Yeah." Morris grasped my hand and pulled me away, stalking down the hall to his office. Opening the door, he pulled me inside and pushed me up against the wall.

"Are you trying to drive me crazy?"

He reached out, gripping my left thigh.

"Depends."

"On what?"

"How many orgasms I get tonight?"

He growled, gripped the bottom of my chin tight, and bit my lip.

"Is that what you're seeking tonight?"

"For your touch. Yes."

"All you had to do was ask."

Morris leaned down, capturing my lips. I raised both arms up, locked them around his neck, and pulled him in close. Lifting me in his arms, sucking and nibbling on my bottom lip, he carried me over to his desk and pushed everything to the floor. I worked fast to unbuckle his pants, helping to remove his jacket and remove my dress.

"Let's... go... to my room." He trailed kisses down my neck.

I shook my head no.

"Here is fine." I squeezed his thick wood through his pants.

His tongue ran across my shoulder, up to my neck. Our eyes never left each other when he extended his hand, releasing my breasts. I thumbed my nipple, squeezing. He bent down, sucking it into his mouth.

"You want this, Lisa." He caught my chin with his index finger.

I planted both hands on his shoulders, holding him in place, squirming. I was so wet and ready to feel him.

"Mmmmm... Morris." I panted as he eased in my opening.

"Hmmm..."

Clenching my thighs around his waist, he thrust and kissed me hungrily, gripping the back of my neck. My eyes closed as he dragged his lips to the curve of my neck, making me shiver in place. I gasped, feeling his girth move faster and faster as our bodies crashed together, tightening my muscles around him.

"Stop... you playing games." A growl spilled out.

"Morris! Yessss... I'm coming."

He pulled out of me and turned me around, forcing me to lie on my stomach. I grasped the edge of the desk, and he slipped back into me.

"Uhhhh... All I ever need." I made an inaudible noise.

"Fuckk!" he groaned behind me, pushing one more time and feeling the condom fill up. I leaned up, fixed my dress, cupped his face, and sucked on his tongue. Morris gripped my ass and held me close in his arms.

"Let's go to your place," he said.

"Maybe another time," I replied, grabbed my purse, and checked my makeup.

"Where are you going?" He gripped me by the elbow.

"Home. I need to work early in the morning."

"So, this was a hit and run?" he questioned.

"Morris, stop thinking like that." I kissed him again on the lips, patted him on the chest, and walked out.

THE NEXT DAY, I WOKE UP BRIGHT AND EARLY TO MEET my contact at a local coffee shop for a story I wanted to tell. Being a reporter, sometimes people looked at me as a threat. Sometimes there were reporters who only looked to exploit people. I prided myself on being the person who rooted out the bad guy and worked for the people without a voice. When everything went down with Maya, I did everything in my power to turn the story around, having them do a new interview with me as a couple—diving into her accomplishments as senator and more. When she decided to run for re-election, the numbers increased for most likely to vote. Then I felt a duty to always tell the truth and be honest above everything else. I put the car in park and took the keys out, making sure I had my recorder and notepad. I got out of the car and headed inside; the young woman was already sitting down. I slid into the booth across from her and smiled.

"How are you, Marisal?"

She scanned the room.

"Nervous."

I reached a hand across the table and patted hers.

"I promise it won't be as bad as you think."

"Are you sure you weren't followed?"

"I wasn't followed; I can make it anonymous."

"I think that's best."

"Sure, let's get started." I removed the recorder from my pocket and put it on the table as the waitress approached.

"Hello, can I get you something to drink?" the short older woman with auburn hair asked.

"Can I get an iced latte and anything she wants?"

"Water is fine," Marisal said.

"Okay, I'll be right back with that," the waitress replied.

I took out my notepad and pen, ready to get the goods on Rhett and his business.

"All right, so tell me exactly what you know about Rhett."

Marisal looked around the shop nervously, and I reached out to comfort her.

"No one knows I'm here, and you're safe."

"He's paying people to push us out," Marisol explained.

"Do you have any evidence?"

"I overheard some guys roughing up a few tenants."

"I will need more evidence before I can go to my boss."

"I'm not getting more involved than I already have."

The waitress came back to the table, dropping our drinks on the table.

"Thank you."

"If he finds out it was me..." Marisal whispered.

"Nothing will happen to you, I promise."

"You don't have a family to worry about."

I sighed, turned the recorder off, and put it back in my coat.

"Look, I can't force you to talk to me. What I'm doing can be dangerous, but it's not just about you and me. We need to get this guy."

"Let me think about it."

"I understand. Here, take my cell phone number and call me if you change your mind." I pulled a business card out and wrote my cell on the back of the card. I hurried out of the booth, removed twenty dollars, and tossed it on the table to pay for our drinks.

"Call me if you change your mind," I called out, and she smiled.

I strolled out of the café and felt around my pocket for my phone, seeing a voice message I missed from my mom. Tommy and Erin were old school and wanted their daughter to go to medical school or become a lawyer. They felt being a reporter wouldn't be real work with too much inconsistency. I took after my mom with my long, wavy, black hair, short, curvy figure, and small button nose. From my dad, I got my attitude and work ethic to always strive for what I wanted even if he disagreed with my career choice.

"Hey, Mommy."

"Why have I not heard from my child?" Mom questioned.

I rolled my eyes, popped the door open, and dropped my bag before putting my seatbelt on.

"Mommy, you know I have to work."

"Work, work, work."

"I promise I will have lunch with you soon."

"Your father is the same way."

"Where's your husband anyway?"

"Your father is playing with his fishing rod."

I chuckled, knowing it pissed her off when she felt ignored by us whenever she wanted attention.

"Leave Daddy alone."

"Get over here soon."

"I will."

"Love you."

"Love you, old lady."

"Bye, child." She ended the call, and I chuckled at her childishness.

I started the car and drove off, heading back to pull an all-nighter on this story.

## LISA

A week later.

Kyla opened the door, and I stepped inside, holding a bottle of wine for our girls' night celebration. Removing my jean jacket, I placed it on the coatrack, kicked off my black ankle boots, and passed her the bottle of wine to open.

"How is filming going?"

I rolled up my sleeves, following her to the kitchen.

"Do you need help with anything?"

"Nope, you're my guest. Have a seat." Kyla grabbed the wine cork out of the drawer, as I reached up for four wine glasses.

"Where's Chelsey and Maya?"

"Should be arriving soon. Maya is at work, and Chelsey is leaving the bank."

"That reminds me... I need to ask Chelsey about opening an account for my goddaughter."

"Which one, Cailey or Amber?"

"Cailey is finally heading to college, and I wanted to get her a gift. As the best godmother in the world, I planned on giving her a bank account with a thousand dollars to start.”

“I don't know what's worse, them being older or us getting old,” she joked, pouring the red wine in the glasses.

“Both.” The doorbell rang, and I hopped out of my seat in the kitchen and ran toward the door.

“Coming! Hold your horses.”

I opened the door, stepped to the side, and gave Maya and Chelsey a hug.

“You both look like you need this more than me.”

“I need the whole bottle,” Maya replied and took the glass out of my hand.

“Well, okay then.”

Chelsey plopped down on the couch and closed her eyes, not saying a word.

“What's up with her?” I whispered to Maya.

“Not sure, she was quiet on the way here,” Maya answered.

“Ummm... Chelsey, you okay, sweetie?”

Chelsey popped one eye open.

“Men,” Chelsey muttered.

“Kyla, grab another bottle; it's going to be a long night,” I called out.

Maya removed her coat and took a seat on the opposite side of the couch from me.

“What do you have to eat, Kyla?” Maya questioned.

Kyla came out of the kitchen with two more glasses of wine on a tray with snacks.

“I have all of your favorites. It's been awhile since we've been together,” Kyla said.

“Good, cause I'm ready to pig out.” Maya gulped the wine down, stood, and went toward the kitchen.

“Chelsey, spill the beans. What's going on?” Kyla asked.

"Work. My father is trying to bring in another manager at the bank."

"I thought you ran the bank." I tucked my feet under my leg, sitting sideways.

"I do, but he still can have a say in things."

"How is your brother doing?" I asked.

"Fine. He's married and a father now," Chelsey answered, picking a cracker and cheese off the tray.

"Tonight is about us unwinding, so no talk about work," Kyla said.

"Wait... did you get the film role?" Maya asked.

Kyla nodded, and their eyes met.

"I did. I'm super excited to be in a meaty role finally and not the sexy girlfriend."

"What about you, Lisa? How are things at the news station?" Maya inquired.

"Good, until I have to curse Ryan out."

"What did he do now?"

"Same old thing, but I have a story I'm working on that could get me in a good position for morning news."

"Okay, now get to the good stuff. I haven't been back to Club Seek, because work is piling up," Chelsey questioned.

"I was there a week ago with Mason," Maya responded, turning music on the radio.

"I have plans to go back sometime this month," Kyla said.

All eyes scanned toward me. I shifted in my seat, not wanting to give myself away at how much I loved being at the club with Morris.

"Someone must have gone recently to be so quiet now," Kyla teased.

"Like last night," I mumbled under my breath and covered my face with my hands.

"I was waiting for you to say something. I overheard

Morris talking to Mason about you."

"That man drives me up a wall." Folding my arms across my chest, I sighed in annoyance.

"I bet money you won't say that to his face," Chelsey joked.

"Girl, no, and risk not getting any. I think not." I laughed, high-fiving Maya.

Kyla jumped up and strolled to the kitchen.

"I'm still surprised you've lasted this long. Lisa, you know relationships aren't your thing," Maya said.

"We're both surprised. I didn't think I would be able to hold out." Kyla brought out another tray of food: wings, pizza, and sushi.

"This all looks good," Chelsey said.

"It's still early, but I have hope he won't give me a reason to dump him."

All three of them burst out in laughter.

"What's so funny?"

"I think we're more worried about Morris than you," Maya responded.

"Morris knows how I feel."

We all looked around, hearing a phone ring. I rose off the couch and grabbed my coat to see it was my phone.

"Hello... Hello."

Not receiving an answer, I hung up.

"Who was that?" Chelsey asked.

"Probably the wrong number."

"Where's Morris anyway tonight?" Kyla asked.

"With my brother and Mason, playing cards."

"Xavier had to work at the gym, and my brother had the baby tonight," Chelsey said.

"Tonight is about hanging out with my girls, and I will do a couple things another day."

"So, tell us about this news story," Maya insisted.

I ROSE OUT OF BED THE NEXT DAY WITH A LIGHT hangover. The girls filled me in on everything that was happening. I was so happy to hear that Kyla received the part she'd been wanting for so long. Chelsey was still dealing with her family's annoyance, and Maya was in the early stages of wanting to run for office again. Today, I had a meeting with Rhett Fuller and wanted to see if he'd admit to the accusations of criminal activity with forcing people out. I strolled out of the bathroom and grabbed my vibrating phone. Seeing Morris' name across the screen, I didn't have time to call him back.

**Morris:** Why didn't you come over?

**Me:** Sorry, I lost track of time.

**Morris:** What are you doing today?

**Me:** I have work and meetings.

**Morris:** We can do lunch.

**Me:** I have a huge story; I can't do lunch.

I dropped the phone on the bed and went to my closet to pick out a comfortable dress suit for my meeting. My phone rang, and I grunted in frustration. I looked back at my phone to see Morris was calling. I hit decline and turned the phone off.

"I'll call him later," I muttered, finished finding something to wear.

An hour later, I arrived at the Fuller Industries office building, showing my ID to security.

"Hello. Do you have an appointment?" She moved the clipboard in front of me, and I looked down, seeing it was for appointments only. I signed my name and nodded.

"Yes, I have an appointment with Rhett Fuller."

"Lisa Reyes."

"That's me."

She typed my information in the computer, and a visitor badge printed out. I attached it to my suit jacket.

"You can have a seat, and someone will be out to escort you back."

"Thank you."

I scanned the front office; it wasn't much to look at compared to other millionaire slimeballs who tried to take advantage of the little people. His taste was more homely style of brown and black colors, with pictures hanging on the wall of him and his staff.

"Lisa Reyes." I heard my name called and glanced up.

"Yes." I stood and followed the young girl through the employee entrance.

"Mr. Fuller is finishing up with a call. You have to go right in and have a seat." She pointed to his open office door, and I thanked her, heading inside. His back was to me, and I stood near the entrance, peering around the room. His office was way different from the front lobby. Everything was marble and silver in color. A table held photos of himself and awards, and a wide window faced the front of the building.

"Miss Reyes, sorry to keep you waiting."

"Huh." I zoned out, not hearing his comment.

"I apologize for leaving you waiting."

"No worries."

"Please have a seat." He motioned toward the seat in front of his desk.

"Thank you, Mr. Fuller."

"Call me Rhett."

"Well, you may not like that after this conversation."

"Oh, what is this about?" He sat up straight in his chair.

"It's about you pushing people out of their homes."

"Who are you with?"

"I'm a reporter."

He jumped up out of his seat.

"Leave."

"Mr. Fuller, I'd think you would want to make it known if you're doing things legally or not."

"Miss Reyes, I wouldn't go down this road if I were you."

He leaned over his desk and pointed his finger in my face. I stood, staring into his eyes.

"I don't intimidate easily, Mr. Fuller."

"My business dealings have nothing to do with you."

"It's about the people you're hurting and leaving homeless."

Rhett hit the call button on his desk.

"Yes, Mr. Fuller?" the receptionist asked.

"Send security up here and escort Miss Reyes out of here."

"No need for security. I'll see my way out."

His nostrils flared, turning bright red with his fists clenched together.

"Right away, sir," the receptionist replied.

A second later, two security guards opened the door, waiting. I grinned, took a business card out of my purse, and placed it on his desk.

"Hopefully, you'll change your mind."

I turned and headed out of his office, with security following. Once out of the building, I looked back at the building, glanced over to the office window, and waved. I slid in my car and drove off feeling excited that I rattled his cage. Peering at the clock on the radio, I saw it was still early and could meet with Morris before I needed to be at the station. I called Kyla while enroute to Morris.

"Hello..." Kyla drew out.

"Are you sitting down?" I asked.

"Uhhh... no."

"What are you doing?"

"At the gym."

"Well, I couldn't wait to tell someone. I just came from Rhett's office."

"Who?"

"Rhett Fuller, the guy I'm doing the story on."

"The millionaire real estate guy?" Kyla questioned.

I stopped at the red light, when all of a sudden, I heard a loud horn behind me, and a car sped past me, with someone cursing me out.

"That was weird."

"What's all that noise?"

"Somebody just drove through a red light."

"Crazy people everywhere. It's Tennessee." Kyla chuckled.

"You're right. I'm almost at the club."

"Kind of early to be at the club."

I bit my bottom lip.

"My energy is on high right now; I need to release some tension."

"Hmm... huh."

I pulled in around the VIP parking area and turned the car off.

"How long are you going to be at the gym?"

"Probably another hour, then I need to run home and study my lines."

I checked my makeup in the mirror, pushed the door open, and glanced around to make sure no one was out.

"Okay, we should have dinner one day this week."

"That's fine. Call me with the details."

"Will do." I ended the call, knocked on the door, and heard the camera moving in the upper-right corner, scanning down on me. Finally, the door opened, and I went back to Morris' office to look for him.

I blew out the candles, tossing the matches on the table, arching a brow, and staring at my beautiful creation. Lisa was held up in a three-sixty spinning swing set, with her legs open, wearing a red bra and thong. We hadn't talked in a few days since our last encounter in my office, and I needed to make things clear before we moved further. My little devil liked to play hard and pretend what we were doing wasn't a full-blown relation-ship. After declining my calls earlier and not showing up at my place the other night, today, she was mine, and I was hers. Her eyes were covered as I approached the bed, ran a hand across her tight ass. To find a woman who loved to be fucked aggressively and worshipped was a breath of fresh air. How she committed to Club Seek and all aspects heightened my desire for her. Hearing her sharp breaths at the lightest touch of my hand, caused my dick to twitch in my boxers. I gripped the head, easing the ache to be inside her to calm down.

"You have me ready to fuck before we talk."

"We can talk afterwards..." She moaned when my finger slid between her thong.

"What did I tell you about trying to run things in here?" I removed my hand and tapped her lightly on the right butt cheek.

"Sorry, sir."

"Good girl." I bent my left knee and climbed up on the bed with my chest to her back.

"Please touch me," she rasped.

"I will in time. First, I want to hear you beg."

I dropped to my knees, turned her around, slid the thong to the side, and brushed my lips against her inner thigh. Moving from the left to the right and pressing kisses, I skimmed my hands up and down her stomach, to her feet as I slid my tongue along her slit.

"Oohh... God." She trembled in my hold.

"I've been waiting all day for this."

"She's ready for you, baby."

Her wetness seeped through and down my chin, nothing like pleasing and hearing her cry out for me to stop torturing with my tongue. The need and want in her voice only encouraged me more. When Maya and Mason first introduced her to me, I didn't want anything to do with this woman. We were both considered dominant, not only in life, but in the bedroom. After our second time together, I made it known that I was in charge by betting I could give her four orgasms in one night. I drove my tongue from her sweet lips to her butt, nipping at each cheek.

"Morris, please!" she yelped.

Pushing my finger in her back door, she gasped at the sensation as my tongue continued sucking her sex.

"She is so wet, baby. Ready for me to own her," I said, removing my finger and letting her have a moment to cool down. I reached over to the chest and grabbed some wipes to clean my hands. Throwing them in the trash and removing my boxers, I picked up a condom and slid him against her lips up to taste. She stuck her tongue out, wanting to taste.

"Will get to that later, baby."

Lining my shaft to her entrance, I eased in slow, nibbling on my bottom lip. She was warm and so tight, I was ready to burst.

"Fuck!" I needed to think of something else before I came too early.

Gripping her by the hips, I moved in slow, gradually keeping my pace so we were both coming undone. Taking my right hand, I grasped her covered right breasts, sucking on her stiff chocolate nipple that I loved to fall asleep against at night.

"Shit, you feel good."

"Ahhh... Sir!"

"You want me to fuck you, baby?"

Nodding her head, I grinned, knowing I was about to wear her out. Biting and licking the pain away, I went to the left breast, holding her in place by the shoulder. I thrust upwards faster. Her breasts bounced up and down, watching them call for another round of my tongue to envelop.

"Damn, you're everything to me, Lisa," I grunted, feeling her juices cover my dick.

"I'm... coming!" she yelled.

"You know better." I yanked out of her, dipped my tongue back inside, closed my eyes, and gripped both her ass cheeks.

WE FINISHED TWO HOURS LATER AFTER GOING FOR A third round on the floor, and I promised to have her again when I got back in town in three days. She reached her wrist out for me to tighten the clasp on her bracelet that fell off.

"Where are you going again?" she questioned.

"It's a new account with a client looking for security at their mall," I said, sliding my navy-blue suit jacket on.

"Why do you have to be gone for three days?" She poked her lips out and frowned.

"We're not together, so why are you questioning me?" Her brow hiked in surprise.

"Morris, don't start." She waved off the conversation and went to grab her shoes from the floor.

"Either we're a couple or not, but you don't get to question me."

She was flushed at my statement.

"I have to get home and work on a story."

"There you go, running out of here before it gets too heated."

"When have I ever run from anything?" She stepped in front of me, and I grabbed her around the waist, pulling her close to my chest.

"You keep the same attitude, see what happens." I kissed her forehead and let her go, and I went back to my office.

KNOCK! KNOCK!

"Yeah."

"I was going through these figures and wanted to get your opinion." Mason stepped in, holding some documents. Being a silent partner, I didn't get involved as much with the day-to-day things about the club. My security company was my primary focus, and I was expanding to Vegas, possibly moving if things worked out in my favor.

"You know I hate looking at numbers."

"Well, too bad. You're part owner." He dumped them on my desk, and I groaned.

"Asshole."

"You packed for Vegas?" he asked.

"Yep."

"I saw Lisa here earlier. Everything good?"

"Fine."

"Something tells me you're not exactly happy with being fine."

I sighed, pushing the forms away from me.

"She's pissed that I'm going out of town."

"It's for work."

"I know that, and I told her, but she's freaked out."

"Headstrong like Maya, and only wants us on their time."

"What did you do to get her as your wife?" I inquired.

"I told her."

I laughed at his words and ran a hand down my face.

"I'll try to remember that."

"Go home or finish working. Take your mind off Lisa and let her come to you," Mason explained.

"I don't know."

"Either you set boundaries now, or you'll be second guessing always." Mason shrugged his shoulders, slid his hands in his pockets, and walked out of my office.

I went through the numbers again, signed off, and made notes on what I would change to make it run smoothly.

Knock! Knock!

"Come in."

"You've been hiding back here all this time," Claire said.

She was a waitress at the club and one time a lover of mine. It was never anything serious, but we became friends. She worked here to put herself through college.

"Guilty," I chortled, sending out an email.

Claire held up a tray with a glass filled.

"Here, I thought you could use this."

"How'd you know?"

"All day, you've been snapping at people." She grinned and sat at the edge of the desk.

"Work stuff."

"You look annoyed."

"I wanted to apolo—" I was surprised at Lisa standing at my office door.

I jumped out of my seat and put the glass down on the desk.

"I see you're busy right now. Have a good flight, Morris," Lisa said as she left.

"Wait!" I yelled, jogging to catch up to her.

"No worries. We can talk when you're back."

"Lisa, stop running." I grasped her arm and nudged her against the car door.

"Go back inside. Your girlfriend is probably mad you're out here with me." She rolled her eyes and looked around, not giving me eye contact.

I smirked. "You're jealous."

"Jealous! Morris, leave me alone." She tried to push me back.

"Claire is a waitress and friend."

"Morris, I'm not stupid."

I gripped her jaw and forced her to face me.

"Claire is nothing to me."

"Then why was she sitting on your desk?"

"So, we question each other now."

"We do when—" she started to say but caught herself.

"What was that?"

"When you're dating someone, and you want a commitment."

"So, is that a yes?"

Lisa looked around the parking lot, bit her bottom lip, and pulled my hand toward her pussy.

"This is a yes."

I cupped her sex, rubbing slowly and kissing along her jawline, as her head fell back on the car door.

"Come with me."

"I can't. I have work on a major story."

"What's the story on?" I lowered my head to her chest, pressed kisses, and moved my left hand up to grab her breast.

"Baby, we can't. People will see."

"Let people watch me touch you and please you."

"Morris! Morris!" We stopped and looked back at Mason who shot daggers at us.

"He started this." Lisa tried to point the blame, and I smacked her on the ass.

"Go home and call me when you make it, so I know you're safe."

"All right, how long are you going to be here?"

"Probably another twenty minutes, then I need to pack before the trip."

"Try to not have too much fun in Vegas."

"Never." I pecked her on the cheek, opened the door to help her slide inside, and watched as she reversed, and headed toward the main street.

"Sorry, bro."

"At least do it away from the cameras," Mason complained, and I laughed. He and I were the only ones with access to the cameras, so he more than likely saw us almost fuck outside. Mason led the way back in the building, went past the bathroom, and saw Claire on the phone. She seemed to be arguing with somebody. She turned away from me and I left it alone, finishing up paperwork.

⌘

THE NEXT MORNING, WHEN I ARRIVED IN VEGAS AT MGM Hotel, I showered and met with potential clients. Barry Lindale owned a chain of smaller casinos, and he was interested in hiring my company to provide security for twenty-four hours. This would lead me to possibly opening an office and moving here.

"Mr. Fields, thank you for coming." Barry extended a hand for a shake. I sat in a chair opposite him.

"When business is called, I run."

"It was nice meeting you at Club Seek."

The waitress poured coffee and left a menu.

"Thank you."

"Order whatever you want. All on me."

"In that case, give me pancakes, scrambled eggs, home fries, and sausage."

"Coming right up," she replied, taking the menu back.

"When did your flight arrive?"

"Around six this morning."

It just turned nine, and my team was waiting for me to brief them on the details.

"After breakfast, we can go over to my casinos."

"How many do you have?"

"Like we talked about, I have about ten casinos, but other businesses as well."

"You want security for just the casinos or everything?"

"To start out, the contract is exclusive for the casinos."

"To cover that amount, I would need to hire more men."

"I saw your background and your experience from the military."

"Most, if not all, of my team is either ex-military, police, or trained by the best."

"Great." Our waitress came over and placed the food down, leaving extra napkins.

"I think you'll like it in Vegas," Barry stated, wiping his mouth, while I sipped on the coffee and started to eat, listening to him work out the details of a contract. A few hours after eating breakfast, we headed to his first casino and did a walk through with my men. I had Warren Kingston tag along to help me scope out any potential details I might miss. Barry talked about the layout of the casino, and I stared over the entire first floor, watching as guests interacted at tables. The place stood on four floors with a stage and entertainment for events on the west side of the building. When high-profile clients came to perform, we'd have to do extra planning for big events.

"He has ten of these casinos?" Warren asked.

"What are you thinking?"

He rubbed his chin in thought.

"Are you planning on moving here permanently?"

I blew out a breath.

"I don't know yet."

"Why? Not like you have anything holding you back home."

I looked at him with a scrunched face. He laughed and slapped me on the shoulder. Warren was like a brother to me; we were both over six feet in height, loved to work out, had large families, and were the oldest among our siblings. The only difference was he has light brown skin, with a low-cut short fade, from New York, whereas I was more athletic in tone. He was muscular and with broad shoulders.

"That look must mean your girl pissed you off."

"It's complicated."

"See, that's why I don't do love."

"The time will come."

"Not too soon, but I like this place. If you want me to help get it off the ground," Warren suggested, pointing to the specs on the blueprints.

"Are you sure?"

"I know you have the club to worry about. Until you make a foolish decision, I can help."

"Thanks, brother." I reached out and gave him a hug and felt my cell phone vibrate in my pocket.

Barry approached us, and I motioned to my phone. Warren took over the tour.

"Hey, Mason."

"Calling to check in and see how things went," Mason asked.

I looked over my shoulder at Barry and Warren talking.

"Things are good. We might have a deal."

"Nice. Just don't forget about the club business once you become a billionaire," he joked.

"My first priority is the club, don't worry."

"That's what I like to hear. We just got approval for another building to expand."

"Email me the information, and I'll look it over."

"Sounds good. See you when you're back," Mason said, and we both hung up at the same time. I finished the rest of the visit with Warren and Barry before we spent the night out on the town. I made a note to call Lisa tomorrow.

## ❧ 4 ❧

## LISA

**T**wo *days later.*

Tonight was my debut story I'd been working on for a few months about a local businessman who was trying to push residents out of their homes to build condos. I'd spent almost a year getting information from residents. Some didn't want to be named, while others were fine with it. I wore my favorite light-blue and cream dress, red heels, and my grandmother's good luck charm bracelet. I ran over the video coverage last night to make sure I had every angle covered. Rhett was doing everything from harassing more tenants, to sending me threats online, and having people call the station to get me fired. Tonight would be the big reveal and hopefully, he'd run scared and get locked up for his crimes. I couldn't be intimated. By the time I was done with him, I could predict I'd end up getting my own show and probably an award for bringing him down.

"Okay, Lisa, you're ready." Frida, my makeup artist, removed the cape.

"Once again, Frida, you've outdone yourself." I stood and checked myself one more time in the mirror.

"Thanks, lady. Good luck."

Production staff stood at the entrance.

"Lisa, five minutes," he said, holding the walkie-talkie in his hand.

"I'm ready." At the beginning, when I found out how the news station played the photos of Maya and Mason, I was ready to give the station management a piece of my mind, but Maya wanted me to stay out of it and not jeopardize my job. If this promotion didn't go my way, then I'd know for sure they were never planning to promote me to my own show. I stepped up on the news desk and let the audio attach a mic to my dress, while I read over my cards.

"Lisa, I'm surprised you're here," Ryan said.

"I'm the cohost of the six o'clock news. Where else would I be?"

"Probably sucking some rich guy dry," Ryan muttered. Our relationship at work was a contest of who could top who in getting the coveted nightly morning news solo spot. When the cameras were rolling, we put on the best friendly atmosphere. Behind the scenes, we couldn't stand each other. Ryan Latchman was a yes man, only out to kiss the boss' ass to get ahead.

"Ready to roll," the director announced in my earpiece. I sat up straight, looked right at the camera, smiled as the light turned red, and the director yelled action.

"Welcome everyone to Nightly CBG News. We have a special report," Ryan said.

"We do indeed, Ryan, and everything has been vetted and approved for air."

"I agree with Lisa, so tonight, our story deals with the latest details on Rhett Fuller."

"They do, Ryan. I personally have worked on this story

for the past few months."

"Do we have the tape?" Ryan asked.

"*Mmmmm... Morris.*" My mouth dropped in surprise.

"*Shit... Lisa, baby.*"

"Wait, is that you, Lisa?" Ryan questioned.

"I...I... This is not."

The video turned off, and I jumped up and ran away to my dressing room. My breath was ragged, my hands shaking, and my eyes watered. I felt nauseous. I covered my face, not understanding how someone was out to get me and switched the tapes. I didn't know anyone was following me, but thinking back over the past few weeks, Rhett was the only person behind sabotaging me.

"Lisa, it's me Frida."

"Go away."

I grabbed my purse, searching for my phone to call Morris. I hadn't talked to him since our little blow up at the club before he went out of town. It was childish to not call him, but I needed time to figure out this mess with Rhett. Now, my head was spinning, and I couldn't believe they'd done the same thing Maya went through. I dialed his number, and the voicemail popped on.

"Lisa, please open the door."

I wouldn't let them see me weak. I wiped the tears away, stood with my shoulders back, and yanked the door open. Frida stood alone with a bottle of water at my door.

"The manager is on his way down now," Frida said, extending the water toward me. I waved it off.

"I'm suing this station."

"First, you need to breathe and take a moment."

She opened the bottled water and forced me to drink.

"I bet this was Ryan."

"He seemed pretty shocked. Most of the team was surprised."

"Somebody knows something."

"What the hell is going on around here!" Taylor, the station manager, barked, stalking into my dressing room.

"That's what I would like to know," I shouted, pointing at the set stage from my room.

"We're getting multiple calls about showing porn on air."

"My privacy was violated!"

"You did it in a public place. I doubt you were looking for privacy," he said sarcastically.

"I want a public apology."

"All of our sponsors are thinking of dropping us, and the station owner wants you to take some time off."

"What!"

"Lisa, you've put me in a bad position."

"My life was just blasted across the world. This has Rhett Fuller all over it."

"Are you still on that story?"

"You don't believe me... typical," I huffed, crossing my arms.

"What I believe is that you need to go and let me try to salvage this station."

"I'm not leaving."

"Then you're suspended. It's not just about you; we have other people who could lose their jobs."

At the mention of other people, I glanced over at Frida and felt a tightness in my chest. I cared about her and the other people who worked at the station. If I put anyone else in a bad spot to lose their job, I'd hate myself.

"I'll leave, but I want an investigation into who did this to me."

"We will let you know. Go home and don't talk to any other media outlets."

"Fine, Taylor." I scooped up my bag and phone, trying

to dial Morris again. I stomped out of the station and kept my head down, not making eye contact when Ryan ran up to me.

"Lisa! Hold up."

"Ryan, you won. I'm on suspension."

"I don't want the position on a technicality."

"How do I know you didn't set me up?"

"You know if I stab you, it's from the front, not behind your back," he said.

I peered at him for a long while, thinking about his words. He was right... Ryan was evil, but he didn't do anything sketchy behind your back if he was coming for you.

"Well, hopefully, Taylor can find out what happened. Sorry about everything," Ryan said.

"Thanks."

❧

IT WAS GOING ON SEVEN AT NIGHT, AND I WAS IN BED with a bottle of wine, lying in the dark with the covers over my head. My phone was on silent, while I searched my name online, saw comments about me being a slut, whore, and slept my way to the top. I went to journalism school and had always been independent. Morris still hadn't responded to my calls earlier, and I wondered if he was pissed off that his business was getting bombarded now.

Bang! Bang!

"Go away!"

"Open this door." I heard Kyla talking to someone on the other side of the door.

"No."

"Lisa, it's Maya. No one more than I can understand what you're going through."

I groaned, threw the cover off me, crawled out of bed, and went to unlock the door. Kyla's face held a harsh glare. Lying back on the bed, I moved the blanket back over my head, and Kyla yanked it out of my hand. A few seconds later Chelsey approached and waved her hand in her face, avoiding the smell.

"Stop hiding and get up." Kyla dropped the comforter on the loveseat in the corner.

"My career is over; my life is over." I reached to the night table to gulp more wine, and Maya snatched it out of my hands.

"Drinking won't help." Maya walked toward the bathroom, and I heard the faucet turn on.

"Okay, so Chelsey, what are you going to do to me?"

She looked around the room, turned the light on, and then opened the blinds.

"Let some fresh air come in. It helps to think clearer," Chelsey replied.

"I don't need an intervention."

"But you need friends," Kyla reminded me and took a seat on the bed.

"It will take a little time for this to go away," Maya explained.

"At least you had Mason to work through the shambles."

"Where's Morris?" Chelsey questioned, and I shrugged my shoulders.

"He hasn't called?" Kyla asked.

"No, and I've blown his phone up for the last few hours," I fussed and checked my messages again.

"Maybe he's still in Vegas," Maya said, which I felt was an excuse she would give since her husband and Morris work together.

"I don't care."

"Yes, you do."

"Shut up, Kyla."

"Get up. We're going out," Kyla said.

"Nope. I'd rather suffer in my room alone."

"This isn't the Lisa Reyes I know," Kyla said.

"Yeah, that Lisa is out of order," I responded and pulled another bottle of wine from under my bed.

"Lisa, give me that!" Maya reached out for the bottle, and I shook my head and ran across the other side of the bed.

"Stop!" Maya screamed and ran to the closet door to hide, and I locked myself in the bathroom.

"Lisa, sweetie, drinking won't help you." Chelsey tried to talk me down.

"Tell that to someone who's not dealing with the world seeing you getting fingered."

"All of us have things we regret," Maya said.

I closed my eyes, took in her words, scanned the bottle of wine, and nodded my head. I went to turn the lock, and they busted in, pulling me in a group hug.

"Where's the fighter who threatened to kick every-body's ass on my behalf?" Maya asked.

"That's different. When it's my family or friends, I become someone else."

"Well, you need that same mentality for yourself. It's not over," Kyla explained.

"Great, you tramps have me tearing up in here, and I hate to cry." I chortled, and they laughed.

"Do you know who has it out for you?" Maya questioned.

"Ohh yeah, Rhett Fuller."

"Who is that?" Kyla asked.

"I've heard of him. A big-time real estate agent," Chelsey answered.

"I was doing a story on him, and I received a few scam

calls but didn't think anything." The girls followed me to my bedroom, and I went into my walk-in closet to grab something to wear for dinner.

"That's how it starts," Kyla said.

"I had one tenant... Marisal."

"Have you spoken to her lately?" Maya typed in her cell phone.

"No, I'll call her tomorrow."

"Just be careful." Chelsey shook her head at me when I held a one-piece jumpsuit up to my chest.

"Let me freshen up." I tossed a short skirt and crop top on the bed, with fresh underwear. I planned on going to find Morris after dinner, to find out why he was ignoring me.

"Maya, do you know anyone who could help me investigate the leak?"

The atmosphere at the restaurant was chilly while we waited for our food to come. At first, I wanted to wear dark shades and hide, but the girls nicked that idea and told me not to hide myself. If Maya could still walk around with her head held high, I knew I could do the same. Tony was still her security, and he sat a few tables away to keep an eye out for anything crazy.

"I can ask Mason, but I think Morris would know better." Maya sipped on her red wine.

"Call Mason," I suggested. Hopefully, he could tell me if Morris was back in town.

"Lisa, I'm not getting in the middle of you two."

"I'm not putting you in the middle," I replied, holding my hands up in surrender.

"Her face looks like she's up to something," Kyla joked.

I flipped her off.

"Please... I just need to confirm something."

She groaned, picked her phone up, and dialed on

speaker.

"Having a good time with your friends?" Mason's deep voice blasted through the phone. Maya's face lit up like a high school girl.

"Hey, babe. Is Malia asleep?" she asked.

"We're still watching *Soul* and painting toenails." Mason grunted, and we heard Malia in the background.

Maya snickered, and I laughed. Mason spoiled Malia rotten, and Maya was more of the disciplinarian when she messed up.

"She needs to go to bed, but we'll talk about it later. Have you spoken to Morris?" she asked.

I shifted in my seat, leaning forward over the table to hear.

"I talked to him earlier today," Mason said.

"Hmmmm..." Maya replied.

"Thanks, Mason," I blurted out and ended the call.

"Lisa! He's going to kill me for hanging up on him," Maya whined.

"Mason's the least of my problems," I remarked, tapped my fingers on the table, leg shaking in nervousness at Morris' behavior.

"You look scared," Kyla said.

"More nervous and curious why he hasn't called me."

"You want to go see him?" Kyla suggested.

"You think they'll let us dress like this?" I inquired, looking down at my outfit.

"All of us showing up wouldn't be good. Maybe just you," Chelsey answered.

"Yeah, I need to go home and make sure my husband isn't pissed," Maya said.

"Or you just want to get home to get some rest while Malia's asleep?" Kyla replied, and they all burst into laughter.

❦ 5 ❦

# LISA

I bumped into a hard chest and almost fell on the floor, but strong hands caught me.

"Sorry about that." I glanced up at the smooth, deep, raspy voice.

The man in front of me was extremely cute, with a wide smile, dimples on both cheeks, and talked like Morris. His light-brown skin matched perfectly with his brown eyes and bushy brows.

"No problem. Ummm... do you know if Morris is here?" I asked.

"He's not here today. I can take a message for you."

"Yeah, can you tell him Lisa was here?"

"You're Lisa... nice," he said.

My eyes dipped in curiosity.

"What does that mean?" I crossed my arms over my chest.

He extended a hand.

"I'm Warren. I work with Morris in his security business."

"Ohh... Well, Warren, it's nice to meet you."

"You too." He winked, turned, and left the lobby. I sighed, wondering where Morris was hiding out and why he hadn't returned my call. Feeling more and more concerned, I went to the bar and got a drink to settle my nerves. I hung out for a few hours before going home and sleeping off the day.

Ring! Ring!

"Hello."

"You should have known not to mess with things you know nothing about," the voice said.

"Hello! Who is this!" I shouted and checked the number, but it came through anonymously.

"Another one for the road?" the bartender asked.

"No, I've had enough for the day." I sighed, placed money on the bar, and left the club.

I got in my car and drove home but made a turn to head to my parents' house to catch up since I missed having lunch.

"The ghost has brought my child home," Dad taunted, holding his arms open.

"Dad, don't start." I reached up and kissed him on the cheek.

"We were worried you left town or something."

I kicked my shoes off and plopped down on the couch. Mother walked up from the hallway.

"She finally remembers who her parents are."

"Hey, old lady," I teased, and she slapped me on the thigh.

"What are you doing here?"

"I just wanted to see you both before I head home."

"Ohhh Lord... it must have something to do with a boy," Dad said.

"Let's not go there."

"Have you met someone?" Mom asked.

"What did you cook for dinner?" I questioned.

"Don't change the subject."

"Mommmm..." I groaned and rose off the couch.

"He must be important for you to be this annoyed." Dad chuckled, leaned over, and picked peanuts out of the candy jar on the table.

"Leave her alone, Tommy."

"Thank you!" I called out from the kitchen, opened the fridge, and picked up a bottle of water.

"Tell me the truth." Mom approached me in the kitchen.

"He's somebody."

"Somebody."

"This is why I don't come here... for the third degree."

"Keep yourself protected."

"No babies coming this way."

"Not just from babies," Mom explained.

"Okay, Momma." I looked over her shoulder at the pot of chili she prepared.

"Are you staying for dinner?" she asked.

"Yeah." I checked my phone again, and there were no messages.

Maybe this was his way of breaking up with me. I chuckled; it was kind of funny since I refused to be in a relationship with anybody. Here's a perfect example of what happened in relationships that weren't anything but headaches. I wasn't the type of girl who got cheated on or lied to; something about being with one person forever felt stifling.

***

The following morning, I felt something off as I slept. Like someone was watching me sleep. I had experience with self-defense, but someone to get in my place without me knowing caught me off guard. I lowered the covers, opened my eyes, glanced from the door to the closet, and felt relief. I was surprised to see Morris sitting in the corner loveseat. He wore a blue blazer, blue slacks, double-breasted suit showing his thick muscles almost bursting at the seams, and his hair was freshly cut. I didn't know if I wanted him to strip out of his clothes or take me out on a date with the way he looked so dapper.

"How did you get in here?" I asked.

"I have my ways."

"No reason for you to be here."

"We won't start the pushing me away a bit."

He stood and stalked toward the bed.

"You can't just stroll in here unannounced."

"I can, and I did."

"Probably was off with your girlfriend."

Morris grabbed my feet, tossed them over his lap, and massaged them.

"How are you doing?" he asked.

"Pissed at you and the world." I shrugged.

"I talked to Maya to get more details."

"Details."

"The video clip of us."

"Are you ashamed?"

"Are you?" He went to massage my thigh, gripping my hand.

"No," I mumbled.

Morris lifted my chin, made eye contact, and kissed me on the lips.

"Don't worry."

"What does that mean?"

"It means Rhett Fuller won't be bothering you."

"Wait, what did you do?"

He stood and walked out of my bedroom. I ran to catch up to him in the kitchen and saw a table filled with food.

"You cooked breakfast?"

"Sit and eat; you're losing what I love about you over stress."

"What do you love about me?"

"Everything." He pecked my lips and poured orange juice in my glass.

"I met Warren last night." I picked up the fork and picked up a strawberry.

"He told me."

"He's cute."

I looked over at his reaction. He stopped drinking his coffee, and I smirked.

"Get your ass spanked."

"Maybe I want to be spanked today."

"Focus on your job first, and that can come later," he explained.

"I'm suspended."

"Do you know who leaked the footage?"

"No, I thought it was Ryan, but I looked into his eyes."

"Hummm..."

"What about someone at the club?" I asked.

"Only people with access are me and Mason."

"Can we just stay home in bed today?"

"No, I have work, and you need to focus on your story."

"Not sure working the story will benefit me anymore."

"That would mean Rhett Fuller wins."

"Maybe he should."

"What happened to the strong, opinionated, feisty woman who takes no bullshit."

I laughed at him.

"I love you."

He stopped eating, stared at me, and leaned forward to slide his tongue inside, and I moaned, feeling tingling at my lower lips. It wasn't time for sex at the moment. He was right, we needed to figure out who's behind getting me pushed out.

❧

Wearing black shades, I followed Morris into his office at his security firm. I never came here because he was always at the club, working alongside Mason. I was shocked at the massive ten-story building and the amount of people who all looked like they were able to bench press a thousand pounds. I licked my lips; the amount of sexiness in the room gave me naughty thoughts I knew Morris would never share.

"Oh, sorry." I bumped into Morris' back.

"That's what happens when you're so busy looking at other people," he growled, grabbing me around the neck to capture my lips in a kiss. I moaned in his mouth and gripped him around the waist.

"How did—" He shushed me with another peck on my lips.

"I know you," I said to the guy sitting at Morris' desk with his feet kicked up.

"You're thinking about me already," Warren joked, winking at me. Morris smacked him on the back of the head, and he stood and chuckled.

"Warren, this is Lisa, my woman," Morris announced.

"Nice to finally meet you formally, Lisa," Warren replied.

"You as well."

"Now that introductions are over, Warren is caught up on your situation."

Warren stood next to my chair.

"I looked into Rhett, and the guy is nothing but a money-hungry leech," Warren explained.

"I know that already."

"Yeah, but he's connected through some nasty people."

"So, what are you saying?"

"We've scoped out his business, and the only way to get him to back off is to play dirty."

"Are you saying kill him?" I whispered, and they looked at each other, then burst into laughter.

"If we told you, we'd have to kill you," Warren replied.

"I don't understand."

"Relax, everything will be fine," Morris answered.

"I trust you."

## MORRIS

A week later.

Every last news channel played the story of Lisa being a member of Club Seek. They talked about her not being respectable and not belonging as a news anchor. I had our tech guy trace the calls that kept hanging up on her, and I found out he worked for Rhett. What I hadn't told her was the person behind the video leak; I needed to brace her for that revelation. Normally, I had men do the following and investigate to get information on criminals, but this was personal. Rhett fucked with the wrong woman this time—my woman. The only thing I could guarantee her was my promise to protect her. Nothing would stand in my way, not even if it meant going to jail. Warren and I laughed at her comment on killing Rhett, but deep down, if he needed to disappear, I could make that happen without batting an eye.

With my connections in security, anyone I loved that was hurt would have my full protection and the problem eliminated. I decided to camp outside his office building alone. Warren was taking my place at the club tonight. I apologized to Lisa for not calling her right when everything happened. I dropped everything when Claire called me about seeing pictures on the news and looked into what happened. Lisa didn't know that I had talked to Ryan and her news station manager, plus other coworkers. Soon as I finished here with making sure Rhett put a stop to all the bullshit, I would show my girl a good time with dinner and a movie. I headed in and saw the secretary talking with another person at the desk. One of my men distracted her as I slipped through the employee door to his office. It was obvious Rhett didn't have too many loyal people since it was easy to pay a few security guards off to give me the layout and hours of him coming and going. I twisted the knob on his office door and pushed it wide open. He jumped up, still holding the phone.

"Who the hell are you?!"

"End the call."

"I'm calling security."

"You probably shouldn't do that if you want to live."

He hesitated for a moment, then finished the call.

"What do you want?"

"You're going to fix the mess you made with Lisa Reyes."

"That bitch!"

I charged at him and pushed him up against the wall.

"Say that again and watch me push my fist down your throat."

"Sorry, sorry. I didn't mean it."

I let him go, smoothing out his suit.

"Here's the problem, Rhett, your underhanded greed is hurting many people."

"I'm a legit businessman."

"No, you're a slimeball."

His eyes rose in shock.

"No need to be shocked. I've done my research."

"You can't prove I had anything to do with her losing her job."

"Do I look stupid to you?"

"Maybe I cut a few strings in business dealings."

"Make it right or find out what I'm capable of doing."

❧

HOURS LATER, I STACKED THE WEIGHTS UP AND STOOD IN front of the mirror, working off the stress from Rhett. Warren invited me to the gym that he and Mason frequented. Come to find out, it was owned by Chelsey's boyfriend Xavier. Lisa ended up going on interviews for other news stations and promised to make up missing dinner plans.

"What happened with Rhett?" Warren marched over to the weight room area.

"He's going to call off his dogs." I raised the fifty-pound weight up to my chest.

"You need me to check in on him." Warren grabbed the towel off his shoulder and wiped the sweat off his face.

"For now, but Vegas is a go. I need you to look into office space."

"I'll handle Vegas and Rhett."

I dropped the weights, bent down, and took a sip from the water bottle.

"Is Xavier here?"

"I guess he's at the other location."

I nodded and gulped the rest of the water down. Hearing my phone go off, I patted my shorts and grabbed my phone to see Lisa on FaceTime.

"You good?" I answered, smiling at her beautiful face.

"Where are you?" she asked.

"At the gym with Warren."

"How long will you be there?"

"Somebody must be missing me?"

She rolled her eyes.

"You're so cocky."

"You home?"

"Yes."

"Meet me at the club in twenty minutes."

"Too stressed."

"I have something that can relieve that stress."

"Is it something that'll put me to sleep?" She lay across the bed, propped her hand under her chin.

"Come find out."

She grinned, and I licked my lips, thinking of what I could do to ease the stress.

"I'll be there in twenty minutes. Don't keep me waiting."

"I promise the wait will be worth it." I bit my bottom lip, ended the call, and turned to see Warren wearing his headphones in the corner, lifting weights. I laughed, slid the phone back in my pocket, and went to let him know I was leaving for the day.

❧　7　☙

## LISA

I pushed the door open, still reeling over getting suspended from work. Being a reporter was the only thing I'd ever wanted to do, and now my career was about to be taken away from me. Maya was helpful, letting me vent to her, but I needed something else to take the pain away. Calling Morris to see if he was here was the only thing on my mind. Normally, you wouldn't catch me out of the house without being dressed up, but today, I only wore a large shirt, tights, and drove fast to get here. Stephen saw how upset I was and allowed me entry even though the rules were not to allow guests unless in all black, upscale attire.

"You've been crying," he stated, standing up from the bed, strolling toward me.

"Terrible day at work."

He wiped the tear away from my cheek and pressed his lips toward mine.

"How did the interview go?" he questioned, running a hand through my loose hair.

"It doesn't matter. I need you."

"Undress."

"I need to feel you, have your arms wrapped around me until I fall asleep."

Morris stood back and watched me undress in front of him. He grasped my hand, closed the space between us, and kissed my lips. It was the sexist thing I'd ever seen. He was so mesmerized or in awe of me. His top lip turned up in a devilish grin.

"What's that look for?"

"I ran you a bath."

"That was sweet."

"Go relax and come back. I have plans for you to take some of the stress away."

Thirty minutes after soaking in the tub, I came out in only a pink silk robe. Morris had a massage table and food laid out for me.

"What's all this?"

"I'm going to help you relax."

"I get a massage."

"Yep, hop on."

Excited, I dropped the robe and climbed on top of the massage table facedown, but he stopped me.

"I want you face up first."

"What type of massage are you giving me?"

"One that will satisfy both of us."

He nudged me on my back, reached over, and picked up a bottle of oil.

"What type of oil is that? It smells good."

"Edible honey cream."

Morris poured a little amount on my stomach, and I felt a cold chill before his warm palm rubbed across my stomach.

"That feels good."

Morris took a small amount and pushed to my lips, and I sucked his finger in my mouth.

"Mmmm... I like the taste."

"Keep sounding like that, we won't get through this massage."

"I'm okay with that."

"In time."

Some of the oil drizzled around my breasts. He bent down and sucked a right nipple in his mouth, and I arched my back off the table. While he made my breast his current meal, I rubbed his back, moved toward his eight-pack chest to a large girth, and reached in his pants to squeeze.

"You relaxed."

"Yes, I need more."

"Your breathing is labored, breasts full, and pussy wet."

"Morris! Ahhh... baby."

As I felt his tongue plunge into my sex, I opened up more for him, and gripped the back of his head. I tossed my head back and forth in pleasure, drenched in my own messiness.

"I'm about to come."

"Hold on."

A few minutes later, I humped his face, and I needed to release and let off my first orgasm as tears pooled in my eyes.

"Let it go," he demanded, pushed both legs back to my chest, and thrust his tongue in my butt.

"Ughhh. Ohhhh... Morris."

Feeling lightheaded and unable to feel my legs, I was ready to sleep from that little bit of pleasure.

"Not so fast." Morris picked me up and turned me around to stand. He kicked my legs apart and slid in my pussy. Part of me tried to scoot away since it was awhile since we last had sex. He knew how large he was, and his slow strokes were just as powerful as his fast ones.

"Oh... yes, Morris," I wailed, gripping the massage table.

He pushed down on my back to right his position, and I felt him slide in deeper.

"You're feeling relaxed!" he taunted, smacking my ass cheeks.

"Yess! Yess. Oh God."

"That's what I wanted to know." He kissed the back of my neck, trailed down my back, and fucked me until we both passed out on the floor, never finishing the food.

❧

"WHAT DID YOU DO LAST NIGHT?" KYLA DIPPED HER sushi in the sauce and took a bite.

"Hung out with Morris." I kept it simple.

She called me to meet up for lunch after she finished with a dress rehearsal. Maya was in DC about some bills, and Chelsey had to work at the bank.

"Hung out or slid in?" she remarked.

"I'll say he helped me relax."

"That glow on your face tells me he did a good job."

I blushed and covered my face with a napkin.

"Anyway, how are things with the job hunt?"

"Slow. I went to some interviews, but I'm still waiting to hear from the station."

"You think they'll fire you for real?"

"Honestly I don't know."

"That's like some HR rule. Maybe get a lawyer."

"I don't plan on giving up so easily."

"That's the Lisa Reyes I know."

"Anything new with your love life?" I asked.

"No, unless you call my favorite toy keeping me warm."

"You ever go to Club Seek like I told you?"

"I don't know if that will be a good idea."

"You can't hold back because of what Maya and I went through."

"Maybe I will, but for now, I'm fine with my toy."

Raising my glass of water, she picked up hers for a toast.

"To our toys." We clinked glasses and laughed in sync.

# MORRIS

A month later.

I scowled at the guy who thought he was in control of any decisions being made. Mason was able to work his magic and spoke with his father to get the legal ball rolling on his properties. Lisa put me in touch with Marisal, and she confirmed with photos and signed notices from residents about the living conditions. A lawsuit was imminent, and criminal charges were filed. The phone calls stopped as soon as we found out they were coming from his own phone with a fake app he had installed. If you're going to be a criminal, at least be a good one and hire out the work. A few blogs still reported on the scandal, but most were removed from their pages, and we were able to get a public apology from some of them for running with the story. She'd been in the business for too long to have her name run through the mud. Rhett, on the other hand, wouldn't back down and tried to run a smear campaign at her station to not hire her back. So, I made a stop today to let him know that his plan wouldn't work. I didn't plan on putting my hands on him, but I knew patience wasn't my friend, so Warren tagged along with me.

I held the yellow envelope in my hand and slid it across the desk toward him.

"What's this?" Rhett asked, picked up the envelope, and held it up in the air.

"Something you don't want out in public."

Warren did what he did best and found photos of Rhett with another woman who wasn't his wife and a small child. I'd bet his wife had no clue he was cheating on her with Frida, the makeup woman at Lisa's network.

"That doesn't prove anything."

"Keep looking."

The smoking gun, a photo of him in bed with her and a tape of them together in bed, and he didn't need any medical care.

"How did you get this?"

"Same way you tried to come for what's mine. I have certain connections as well."

"I did what you said and put a stop to the calls."

"But you're still trying to ruin Lisa's name at work."

"She got in the way!" he shouted.

"No, your ass is just plain fucked up for having people live in terrible conditions."

He started to cry, and I didn't feel sorry for him.

"You have twenty-four hours, or I'm showing your wife and the media."

"Listen, I can pay you whatever you want."

"I don't want your money. Turn yourself in and send an apology to Lisa."

"I can't go to jail!" he shrieked.

"Whose problem is that?"

"Okay, wait... maybe we can negotiate," Rhett pleaded, dropped to his knees in front of me.

"You may want to save the begging for your wife." I turned and left the office, while he continued to call my name.

⚜

I SMELLED HER BEFORE SHE EVEN WALKED IN THE kitchen; her floral and lavender scent flowed in the air. It was my favorite shower gel on her that I continued to buy whenever she stayed overnight.

"What are you cooking?" She dropped her bag on the counter and hugged me around the waist. I stirred the spicy, tangy sauce for the hot wings and fries I was making for dinner tonight; it was one of her favorites. Living in a three-bedroom house alone without someone to come home and cook for left me empty. The way Mason embraced being a husband and father was something I admired. Now, after everything Lisa and I went through, I needed to know we were on the same page with what we wanted out of this relationship.

"Taste this sauce." I held the wooden spoon up, and she pulled her hair to the side, to keep it from getting in the sauce.

"Hot and spicy like you," she said, leaning into a kiss.

"I have your favorite wine, if you want to wash your hands for dinner."

"Something must be serious for you to have my wine ready."

"I'd rather have you drunk before I spill this news."

"You're scaring me now."

"First wash up." I turned the oven off and removed the apron before turning to kiss her on the forehead. She was hesitant but finally left the kitchen to clean up. I fixed our plates, opened her wine, and set everything on the table, along with the photos. Warren sent a message that he tracked Rhett meeting with his attorney, then heading to the police station. Only a matter of time before Frida quit and skipped town.

"I'm back, so tell me."

"Sit first and have a glass of wine."

"Morris, I'm not a child. I can handle whatever you have to say."

"Are you sure?"

"Yes. Now what is going on? Are you breaking up with me?" She jumped out of her seat.

"No, sit and eat, so I can explain."

Her slanted eyes watched as I picked up my glass and drank.

"I signed a deal to do work in Vegas."

She gasped in shock.

"You're moving."

"No, not yet anyway. Possibly in a few months."

"Then why did you declare this love and want to make a commitment?"

"I haven't decided if I'm moving, and I have people who can handle my company."

"I knew this was a setup." She gulped her wine down and slammed the glass on the table.

"Stop thinking the what-ifs. I wouldn't just up and leave without consulting with you." She sucked her teeth. "Anyway, that's not what I want to talk about; it's not that important."

"You moving is important."

"Woman, shut up!" I shouted, and she froze and rolled her eyes.

"Not your woman," she murmured slowly.

"Keep pouting, and you'll have something other than this to eat on tonight."

She smiled at my statement, and I chuckled. She was spoiled and entitled, but it was all my fault.

"Rhett is having an affair with Frida, and she leaked the footage," I blurted out, and her mouth dropped open in surprise.

"Frida who?"

"Frida, the makeup artist you work with, babe."

"Morris, I need you to back up and explain."

"Warren did some digging for me on Rhett Fuller, and he was the one doing the phone calls from a fake app, and he had Frida get the fake tape on air," I explained.

Lisa dropped her head in her hands, and I scooted the chair back and went to lift her out to sit on my lap.

"That bitch," Lisa yelled. She tried to get out of my hold, and I tightened my grip.

"Lisa, you're not fighting."

"Like hell I'm not. Let me go."

"Baby, let me handle things. I promised, and I delivered on my promises."

Lisa stopped fighting me and dropped to the ground. I picked her up and carried her to the bedroom upstairs.

"She's been smiling in my face and pretending to have my back."

"Rhett probably promised that he would marry her and leave his wife."

"Wait, she has a kid?" she questioned.

I kicked my bedroom door open and placed her down, moving the pillows off the bed.

"Relax and get some rest. We can talk more after you've had some time to yourself." I tried to get up and leave, but she gripped my arm.

"Please stay and hold me."

Her pouty lips begged to be kissed, but now wasn't the time for sex.

"I'll stay until you fall asleep."
"You keep me protected," she said.
"You keep clear."

Three days later.

After ending a call with Marisal, I watched the news talk about Rhett Fuller being indicted on charges and his attorney trying to get him out on bail. I was still suspended, but I decided to come up to the station and cause a fit. My attorney had the papers drawn up and ready to file a lawsuit. I decided to not sit and dwell on what I couldn't control, so I jumped in my car and drove here to the station. Morris had no clue. We'd spent time at his house for the past three days, and I even had clothes in his closet. He had to fly back to Vegas two days ago and came back today. We'd be together for dinner tonight.

I waved my badge, and security allowed me in even though I wasn't supposed to be on the premises. I caught Frida leaving work and kicked her ass for helping Rhett. Taylor threatened to call the police on me. Frida tried to apologize, but she made her bed with the devil. Her money train was cut off; the wife knew about the affair and made sure to cut Rhett off from everything. Frida got fired, and I didn't feel bad at all for her child. The devil was in the details.

"What are you doing here?" Ryan asked.

I looked around the station, and the crew was moving cameras and dollies around, getting set up for the next segment.

"I came to see Taylor."

"Does he know that?"

"Ryan, either you're friend or foe."

"Not my business." He stood to the side, and I swished down the hall toward Taylor's office. I just happened to see the door open and saw two other men in his office, looking just as upset. One was Dimitri, the owner, and the other was his assistant, I believe.

"Lisa, what are you doing here?" Taylor questioned. My head cocked slightly to the side. Keeping my life on hold wasn't a high priority for him. Everyone in this station knew I was the fan favorite with the audience, and the ratings had dropped over the past few days.

"I'm here to find out when I'm back on air."

"It's not a good time."

"Why? I think now is the perfect time. I mean you've allowed my reputation to be destroyed and continued to allow Frida to work here even after finding out what she did."

"Lisa." Taylor's breath hitched.

"Here's what I'm going to do. You can either put me on for Friday, with a raise and two-week vacation, or a ten-million lawsuit will be at your door before I leave this building."

Taylor and I stared at each other.

"Lisa, we understand what has gone on and owe you an apology," Dimitri Carruthers explained.

"Mr. Carruthers," Taylor spoke.

"No, Taylor, you've done enough. Give her whatever she wants," Dimitri ordered.

"Thank you, Mr. Carruthers." I smirked, extending a hand to him, then Taylor. I couldn't blame him for being upset, but he messed with the wrong woman.

❦

I SPOTTED FRIDA WITH TWO BAGS OF GROCERIES, arguing with someone on the phone, and I bet it was Rhett. I jumped out of the car, removed my shades, glanced at the car door still open, and walked over to see a baby boy in the back, playing with a teddy bear.

"Are you here to fight again?" Frida asked.

She reached in the car and grabbed her son, heading to her front door.

"Why?"

Frida looked at the ground.

"I thought we were friends."

"Look, Lisa, I didn't mean for this to happen."

"But you knew how much my career meant to me."

"I had to do what's best for my child."

"I guess you can't find loyalty anywhere."

"You got what you wanted. You're more famous now," she snapped back.

"Frida, you're lucky your child is here right now." I clenched my fist at my sides at her nonchalant attitude.

"Rhett's in jail. I'm broke and about to move in with my family," Frida informed me, and I didn't care. She brought this on herself.

"Too bad, so sad." I gritted my teeth, left to go home to my man and grab another session if he was at the club.

Driving, I called the girls on the way through Bluetooth.

"What happened?" Kyla asked right away.

"Did you get your job back?" Chelsey questioned.

"Yes, they didn't want a lawsuit on their asses." I slowed at the red light.

"Same hour slot?"

"Yeah, then I went to see Frida again."

"You didn't fight her again, did you, Lisa?" Kyla questioned.

I giggled and pulled off when the light turned, heading on the freeway toward downtown.

"No. Her son was there."

"Thank God," Chelsey muttered.

"Since that's over, did you talk with Morris about Vegas?" Kyla brought up, and I didn't know how to answer that question.

"Not yet."

"Has he made a decision?" Kyla inquired.

"Right now, Warren is handling everything."

❦

FIFTEEN MINUTES LATER, I ARRIVED AT THE CLUB AND parked around back in the VIP reserved area.

"I'm about to see him now. Let me call you tomorrow."

"You're at the club?" Kyla questioned.

"Maybe."

"Have fun," Kyla joked.

I ended the call, checked my makeup in the mirror, and sprayed some perfume on my wrist and neck. As I hopped out of the car, I checked my outfit over, sauntered to the door, and released a breath before I knocked.

## LISA

"Keep your eyes forward." He lifted the remote and clicked a button. The wall slid open to a TV screen. I sat butt naked on the bed with my legs cocked open.

"Morris..." My breathing was desperate at seeing him between my legs, eating me out. One of my favorite things I liked was to watch us together, making little movies of our escapades brought me excitement and joy.

"I want you to watch us on the screen, while I eat you out."

Whap!

He spanked me on the ass, flipped me on all fours, and spread my legs wide.

"You're not allowed to touch me or come until I say so," he demanded.

"Awwww!!!!" I panted and reached back to grip Morris by the back of his head.

"Don't take your eyes off the screen," he said.

The clip showed Morris with a flogger going across my breasts. I licked my lips, thinking of that night together.

Listening to my cries and pants of how much I busted in his mouth when he double penetrated me with the vibrator and his dick.

"Please..." I gasped, rocking back and forth.

"You want to come."

"Aghhh..." I yelled and felt my heart pounding. I would miss having these moments if he left for Vegas full time. His fingers pushed through my walls, pistoned in and out, repeatedly.

"Shhh..." Morris trailed kisses up my back, yanked my head back by my hair, and rushed to thrust back in with his large girth. "Fuck!" he croaked, moving in long strokes, and pushed me flat on the bed, holding my hands tight behind me.

A strangled cry was on the tip of my tongue as sweat dripped down on the sheets and makeup smeared all over.

"Ughhh... Shit."

There was nothing simple about this sex session beyond him defining what we meant to each other. I trusted him without a doubt. We'd be together forever.

"Ahhhh... I'm about to come."

"Let it go," he replied, speeding up his pace as slid his hand underneath, playing with my clit.

"Fuckkk!" I screamed. I felt his hands release my arms and grip the sides of my waist to catch his orgasm.

He fell on the side of the bed with his hand over his eyes. I moved my hair behind my ear, scooted over, and planted a kiss on his chest up to his lips. He wrapped a hand around my waist and snuggled his face in my neck.

"That was amazing."

"Glad you're satisfied," he replied.

I grinned, lifting my hand to run a finger on his pink, full, bottom lip.

"Have you decided about Vegas?" I didn't want to make

this awkward, but I needed to know where we would stand in a few weeks.

"Warren and I will rotate and fly back and forth to Vegas."

"A new business needs a manager at all times."

"We have someone who'll be there at all times, but I'll need to check in on them."

We gazed into each other's eyes, and I thought about the first time we met. I was having lunch with Maya, and he was with Mason. Our first meeting wasn't the best, and I thought he was an asshole. Life had a way of showing you the love of your life could be in the form of the most challenging man.

"Come with me to Vegas," he suggested, moving to grab the remote and turn the TV off.

I sat up and wrapped the sheets around my body.

"I can't. I have to work this week."

"You have your job back?" he questioned, and I nodded. "After you finish work, we can fly out for the weekend."

"What are we going to do in Vegas besides gambling?"

"Anything you want, love." I chuckled at his response. "I like hearing that from you."

"Spoiled ass." He smirked, rubbed my ass, lifted me out of the bed, and I dropped the sheets on the floor.

"Tonight, you're all mine." He growled, sucked my bottom lip, and carried me to the bathroom.

❧

THE WEEKEND IN VEGAS.

"How much are you going to put on her, Morris?" Kyla asked, laughing at Morris. My girl came out with me to Vegas so I could have company while he worked with Warren. We've already gone shopping and gambling, so we ended up at the pool in our bikinis, lying under the sun. Chelsey and Maya had to work and FaceTimed us earlier. Next time they were free, we would all fly out together.

"As much as I think she needs." Morris grunted, and I chuckled as they went back and forth like brother and sister. He was a perfect gentleman and didn't allow me to pay for anything when we arrived and had us in the suite for the entire weekend.

"He hasn't taken his hands off you since we've been out here," Kyla said, grabbing her margarita to sip.

"Kyla, leave him alone." I laughed at the scowl on his face.

"Oh, calm down, crazy man. You've run all the guys away," Kyla fussed, and he kissed my forehead.

"Good," he said.

"Morris, I got Barry on the phone wanting to talk to you." I glanced up as Warren approached us.

"Hi, Warren," I said.

"What's up, brat?" he teased, nudging me playfully.

Morris took the phone from Warren's hand and stepped near the empty cabana for privacy.

"Kyla, you remember Warren, right?" I introduced them, and they stared at each other.

"Ummm... hey," Kyla said.

"What's up?" Warren responded and went to walk toward Morris.

"What was that?" I asked.

"Huh."

"You two just eye-fucked each other," I whispered.

"Lisa, please," Kyla chortled.

"I'm just saying we're here for the weekend—nothing wrong with a one-night stand."

"No, thank you. Men and relationships aren't on my agenda," Kyla explained.

I raised a glass, Kyla picked up hers, and we toasted.

"Then maybe you should try out Club Seek when we get back."

"Hmmm..."

"The best place to be." I laughed, took a sip of my drink, and watched my man talk with his friend. I thought of all the fun we would have later tonight.

## EPILOGUE MORRIS

One year later.

I stood in the corner as Lisa sat at the anchor desk of the CGN Morning News, doing a segment on the latest oil industry. Our relationship had grown deeper and more intense as we balanced our lives together. Recently, her parents came out to Vegas to stay at the casino where I worked security, and they fell in love with the place. We had dinner the other night to celebrate her new gig as solo anchor. Our nights at the club had slowed down because our work schedules increased. I still went back and forth between Vegas and Tennessee every other month, so I built our very own sex club in my house. She finished her segment and when the camera was off, we clapped as balloons and a cake came out. Her growth only inspired me more, and I opened another security business location in Chicago and worked with Mason on opening a club out there. Warren stood next to me and stared at Lisa hugging her friends.

"I'm assuming you're only looking at Kyla."

"What?"

"She's the only single one left."

"I'm not looking at her."

"Uhhh."

"Unlike you and Mason, I'm not into love and answering to somebody."

"Welp, you're missing out." I laughed. Lisa placed her hand on my chest.

"Hey, handsome," Lisa purred, pursing her lips for a kiss.

"Congrats again, Lisa," Warren said.

"Thanks, Warren."

"Are you ready for lunch?"

"Can we make it a big lunch? I invited the girls."

"Sure."

"Great. I want a huge glass of red wine."

"Sure, babe."

"Warren, are you coming to lunch?" Lisa asked.

He raised his wrist and looked at his watch.

"Not this time, brat. I have to get to the office," Warren responded, reaching over to hug her.

"Shut up, Warren." She rolled her eyes.

He chuckled and walked off.

"Can we go to my office?" Lisa whispered in my ear.

"No."

"Why not?" She pouted.

"Because I'll be here all day."

"Lisa, we're not about to wait on you so you can get some dick," Maya murmured, and Kyla laughed.

"With friends like you three, I'd never get away with anything." Lisa huffed. I held the door open for the women to head toward the parking lot.

"Good," I responded, kissing her on the forehead.

I hope you enjoyed Lisa and Morris story. Please also check out **"Seek To Bare Book 3" here** https://books2read.com/u/mvoKDz with Kyla and Warren. Some of your favorite characters appear.

Did I forget to mention the final installment of Xavier and Chelsey with **"Seek To Love Book 4"** is here https://books2read.com/u/mB2QvO

Check out Brother's BestFriend Romance here ***"Sensual"*** https://books2read.com/u/49lYYM

Don't miss out on ***"Love Don't Live here Anymore book 1"*** https://books2read.com/u/mBOWGZ a steamy enemies to lovers romance.

Have you checked out **"His Peace Her Pleasure"** click here https://books2read.com/u/3JJroP a billionaire, steamy romance.

# WHAT'S NEXT

WANT TO KNOW WHAT HAPPENS next?

Follow me on Bookbub and social media today.

Reviews are the lifeblood of the publishing world. They're read, appreciated, and needed. Please consider taking the time to leave a few words on wherever you buy books. Sign up for updates and sneak peeks at the site below.

I WANT TO THANK FIRST readers for loving these characters so much and waited so love for them to come back.

# ACKNOWLEDGMENTS

I CAN'T MENTION ENOUGH the support and dedication of my author buddies for keeping me uplifted. My behind-the-scenes team of beta readers, editors, designers, and more. As a writer, I continue to strive for the best, and I appreciate everyone who reads my work. Without your continual feedback, I wouldn't be on this path, letting doubts slip away.

# ABOUT THE AUTHOR

A Tennessee native and CA dreaming Author Keke Renee is living and striving to continue her passion of writing Short Story romances from Erotic, Women's Fiction, Romantic Suspense, Paranormal and Urban fiction.